BLOOMSBURY
PAPERBACKS

D1479892

THIS BLOOMSBURY BOOK

BELONGS TO

....

For Imogen & Phoebe, with love
R.H.

For Smriti, who asked me to do the book
B.C.

Bloomsbury Publishing, London, Berlin and New York

First published in Great Britain in 2008 by Bloomsbury Publishing Plc
36 Soho Square, London, W1D 3QY

This paperback edition first published in 2009

A CIP catalogue record of this book is available from the British Library

Designed by Ian Butterworth

ISBN 978 0 7475 8757 6

Printed in China

1 3 5 7 9 10 8 6 4 2

All papers used by Bloomsbury Publishing are natural, recyclable products
made from wood grown in well-managed forests. The manufacturing processes
conform to the environmental regulations of the country of origin

www.bloomsbury.com/childrens

If I Were You

Richard Hamilton

Illustrated by

Babette Cole

BLOOMSBURY

LONDON BERLIN NEW YORK

Dad tucked Daisy up in bed.

"He said, "If I were you, I'd snuggle down and go to sleep."

"But you're not me," said Daisy.

"I know . . . but if I were," Dad yawned.

And that set Daisy thinking . . .

"If you were me and I were you," Daisy said,
"I'd read you a story about **three bears** . . .

then I'd say 'goodnight'
and go downstairs!"

"If you were me and I were you," said Dad,
"I'd go to sleep with Kangaroo,

and in the morning **bounce on you!**"

"If you were me and I were you," said Daisy,
"I'd dress you in a **pink tutu!**

I'd give you breakfast ... **porridge,** every day ...

while I had chocolate fromage frais!"

Dad sat up and stroked his chin.

"If you were me – now let me see –
while you washed up, I'd watch TV!

Then I could play with Millie the mouse,
while you made beds and tidied the house!"

Daisy wasn't sure about that!

She said, "Then we'd go out for some fresh air!
And I'd push you in my old pushchair."

"What?" said Dad.
"Past the neighbours? Dressed in pink?
Can you imagine what they'd think?"

"If I were you and you were me," said Daisy,
"I'd take you to the zoo to see
the baby elephants and cheetahs,
the crocodiles and anteaters!"

Dad clapped his hands and said,
"Could we go by bus and buy balloons?
Eat ice creams and see baboons?"

"Yes, if you were very, **very** good," said Daisy,
"and behaved **exactly** as you should."

"And after the zoo, could we play in the park,
and stay out till it's really dark?"

Daisy folded her arms.

"We could go to the park but not for long . . .
You're so heavy and I'm not that strong."

"After the park I'd give you tea,
with your friends and Mummy and Baby and me.

And you could play games like musical chairs,
and pass the parcel and hunt the bears."

"And then a bath to make me clean,
with ducks and bubbles and submarines?"

"I'd make you wash your face and hair,
behind your ears . . . everywhere!"

"And then I'd tuck you up in bed,
and give you a big kiss on your head."

Dad sighed, "What a day! I'd think I was dreaming —
no washing, no cooking, no driving, no cleaning!
Wouldn't it be great?"

Daisy looked at her dad.

She said, "Dad, if I were you and you were me . . .

... I think I'd rather be me!"

Enjoy more fantastic Bloomsbury picture books . . .

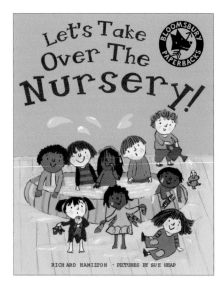

Let's Take Over The Nursery!

by Richard Hamilton
& illustrated by Sue Heap

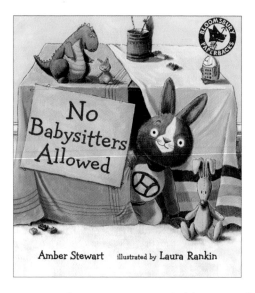

No Babysitters Allowed

by Amber Stewart
& illustrated by Laura Rankin

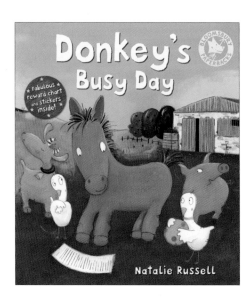

Donkey's Busy Day

by Natalie Russell

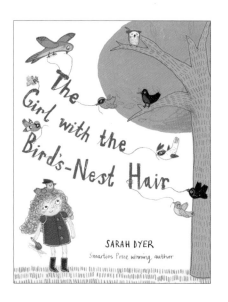

The Girl with the Bird's-Nest Hair

by Sarah Dyer